Twin
Trouble

Jacqueline Wilson

illustrated by **Philippe Dupasquier**

mammoth

Also by Jacqueline Wilson
in Mammoth Storybooks

Connie and the Water Babies

First published in Great Britain 1994
by Methuen Children's Books Ltd
Published 1995 by Mammoth
an imprint of Egmont Children's Books Limited
239 Kensington High Street, London W8 6SA

Text copyright © 1994 Jacqueline Wilson
Illustrations copyright © 1994 Philippe Dupasquier
Cover illustration copyright © 1999 Claire Tindall

The moral rights of the author, illustrator and cover illustrator have been asserted.

ISBN 0 7497 1985 0

3 5 7 9 10 8 6 4

A CIP catalogue record for this title
is available from the British Library

Printed in Great Britain
by Cox & Wyman Ltd, Reading, Berkshire

Contents

1 Double Shock

'We've got something wonderful to tell you, Connie,' said Mum.

'You're going to be so thrilled,' said Dad.

Connie blinked at them both. Their faces were pink. Their eyes were shining. They weren't teasing.

'What? What, Mum? What, Dad? Tell me!' said Connie.

'Can't you guess?' said Mum.

'It's what we've always wanted,' said Dad.

Connie's heart started thumping inside her T-shirt.

'Oh, Mum! Oh, Dad! Are we going to Disneyland?' she said.

Mum and Dad blinked back at her.

'What?' said Mum. 'Oh, Connie, this is better

than a trip to Disneyland.'

'Better than seeing Mickey Mouse?' said Connie, doubtfully.

'Mickey Mouse is only pretend. This is real,' said Dad.

'Am I getting a real mouse?' said Connie, perking up. 'Can I have a white one, please? And a black one too? And then they could maybe have babies, and they might come out in black and white stripes like very weeny zebras.'

'Do stop burbling, Connie,' said Dad. 'We're not talking about mice having babies. It's Mum.'

'Mum?' said Connie. 'Mum's having baby mice?'

Oh, Connie,' said Mum. 'I'm having baby *babies.*'

'Baby babies?' said Connie. She didn't just sound doubtful now. She looked it too.

'Don't look so worried,' said Mum, laughing. 'I'm not having lots and lots. Just two. Twins.'

'Isn't it marvellous?' said Dad, and he gave Connie a little nudge so that she'd say yes.

Connie didn't say anything. She was thinking. She wasn't sure she liked babies very much. Connie's best friend Karen had a baby sister called Susie. Susie looked sweet enough, but when Connie had picked her up to give her a cuddle

Susie had been sick all down the front of Connie's best teddy bear jumper. Connie had never been very keen on Susie after that. Come to think of it, Karen wasn't very keen on Susie either. She screamed a lot. That was just one baby. Two would be twice as bad.

'Hey, Connie!' said Dad, giving her another nudge. 'You know how we've always longed for more children.'

'Have we?' said Connie.

'That's why I had all that special treatment at the doctor's,' said Mum. 'So I could give you a baby brother or a baby sister, Connie. And now I can give you both all in one go.'

'It's going to get a bit crowded round here then,' said Connie. 'Where are they going to sleep, these twin babies?'

Mum and Dad looked at each other. Connie started to get suspicious.

'They're not going to come in with me, are they?' she said. 'There won't be room for three of us.'

'That's right,' said Dad. 'So Mum and I have had this really good idea.'

'What?' said Connie. She wasn't so sure about Mum and Dad and their ideas now.

'We thought we could make you a special new

big girl's bedroom,' said Mum. 'Then the twins could have your old room.'

'A new big girl's bedroom?' said Connie slowly. She thought about the extension at the back of her friend Karen's house. 'Ooh, are we going to build an extension?' she said hopefully, imagining a huge glass room jutting right out into the garden.

'Come off it, Connie, you know we couldn't afford it,' said Dad, and he sounded a bit grumpy. 'First it's Disneyland, then it's extensions. We're not made of money, you know. And when we're a family of five we'll have to be really careful with our money.'

Connie wasn't at all sure she wanted them to be a family of five. They'd managed beautifully in the past being a family of three.

'We thought the junk room would make you a lovely new big girl's bedroom,' said Mum.

'The junk room!' shrieked Connie. (She didn't actually say it. She shrieked it.)

There were three rooms upstairs, not counting the bathroom. There was Mum and Dad's bedroom. There was Connie's bedroom. And there was the little junk room at the front of the house. It was called the junk room because it was jammed up with junk; suitcases and an old broken sofa; cardboard boxes of books and an old bike;

11

and heaps of toys that Connie didn't want to play with any more. Connie was starting to feel like one of the tired old teddies or droopy dolls. Mum and Dad seemed to have got fed up playing with her. They wanted a shiny new set of twins now. It was time to shove Connie in the junk room.

2 Name Games

Connie thought she might have to balance her bed on top of all the junk in the junk room and sleep crammed against the ceiling. But Mum and Dad sifted through all the junk and threw a lot of it out. When the room was bare they painted it deep blue and stuck shiny stars up on the ceiling. Mum made Connie a new pink and blue patch-work quilt to go on her bed and Dad made shelves all the way up one wall for Connie's books and games and videos. By the time they were finished it certainly wasn't a junk room. It was a beautiful big girl's bedroom.

Connie couldn't help but be pleased, but she still didn't like seeing her old bedroom turned into a nursery for the twins. They didn't just have new paint and a new quilt and new shelves. They had new everything. Twin cots. Twin pram. Twin baby chairs. The twins weren't even here yet and already they seemed to be crowding Connie out.

Mum was getting big and tired and needed lots of rest. She couldn't dance to pop videos with Connie any more and sometimes when she was reading a bedtime story she nodded right off to sleep as she was speaking.

Dad was getting worried about money and kept doing sums on bits of paper and sighing. He didn't often feel like having a tickling match with Connie nowadays and didn't go swimming with her on Saturday mornings because he was working overtime.

'It's not any fun round here any more,' Connie said darkly. 'It's all because of those boring babies. Who wants to have twitty old twins anyway?'

'We do,' said Mum, firmly. 'Come and give me a cuddle, Connie.'

Mum was very big indeed now but Connie managed to squash into a corner of the sofa beside her.

'You'll like your baby brother and sister when they're here,' said Mum.

'Will I?' said Connie.

'And you're going to be a super big sister and

help Mum look after the babies, aren't you, Connie?' said Dad.

'Am I?' said Connie.

'What are we going to call these twins, eh?' said Mum. 'Have you got any good ideas, Connie?'

Connie had called the babies all sorts of names to herself. They were generally rather rude names. It wasn't a good idea to announce these to Mum and Dad, so she simply shrugged.

'Come on, Connie, you choose,' said Dad. 'Think of two names that go together.'

'Mickey and Minnie,' said Connie.

Mum and Dad didn't think a lot of this suggestion.

'Chip and Dale? Laurel and Hardy? Marks and Spencer?' said Connie.

'Stop being silly, sausage,' said Mum, tweaking Connie's nose. 'How about two names that go with *your* name?'

Connie thought hard. 'Bonnie and Ronnie?' She thought this a brilliant idea. She wasn't being silly at all. But Mum and Dad were not keen. They decided on Claire and Charles. Connie thought these very boring names. But then she thought these were very boring babies.

Weeks and weeks went by and Connie was fed up waiting for the babies to arrive. But then one night Granny came to stay and Dad took Mum to the hospital. Dad didn't get back until breakfast and then he gave Connie a big hug, Granny a big hug and, when the postman knocked at the door, he very nearly gave him a big hug, too.

'It's twins!' he said, as if it was a big surprise. 'A lovely little boy and a lovely little girl. Charles and Claire – a perfect pair!'

'I'm Connie alone. One on my own,' Connie muttered.

'What's that, Connie?' said Dad. 'You want to see your little brother and sister eh? Granny will meet you after school and take you to the hospital.'

It was good fun at school showing off about the twins. Connie told Karen and all her friends; then she told the teacher and was allowed to write on the blackboard: CONNIE HAS A NEW BABY SISTER AND BROTHER. She did a picture of them too, with pink chalk and yellow for their curls. She wasn't sure what they looked like yet but all babies looked more or less the same, didn't they?

She got a shock when Granny took her to the hospital. There was Mum lying back in her bed, little again and looking very happy. There were two cots at the end of Mum's bed and there was a baby in each cot.

'Oh, aren't they *sweet!*' Granny cooed. 'Oh, what perfect little pets. The pretty little darlings!'

Connie didn't think the twins looked sweet or perfect or pretty. They were certainly little. Much smaller than she'd expected. Tiny weeny wizened little creatures. They didn't look a bit like Karen's baby sister Susie. They didn't even have any hair. Not one curl between them. They were as bald as Connie's grandpa – and much uglier.

'Aren't you lucky to have such a lovely baby brother and sister, Connie?' said Granny.

Connie didn't feel lucky at all.

3 Wailing Whimpers

It got worse when Mum and the twins came home from the hospital. Granny and Grandpa and all sorts of aunties and assorted friends and neighbours came crowding into the house, too. They pushed past Connie, barely giving her a nod. They rushed over to the twins and then they started gurgling and giggling and goo-goo-gooing. (Not the twins. Granny and Grandpa and all the aunties and assorted friends and neighbours gurgled and giggled and goo-goo-gooed.)

The twins didn't respond. Sometimes they slept through all this attention. Most of the time they whimpered and wailed. For such tiny little creatures they could make an immensely loud noise.

'Hark at them exercising those little lungs,' said Granny, knitting busily.

She was knitting a tiny pink teddy bear jumper for Claire and a tiny blue teddy bear jumper for Charles. She didn't seem to have time to make a new teddy bear jumper for Connie even though Connie had explained that her old teddy bear jumper had never been the same since the mishap with Karen's sister, Susie.

'I'd rather like a pink teddy bear jumper,' said Connie. 'Or would I like blue better? I know! How about pink and blue striped. With a yellow teddy bear.'

'What's that, dear?' said Granny vaguely. 'I can't quite hear you.'

'Because the twins are making such a racket,' Connie said, sourly. 'They're giving me a headache.'

'It's just their way of saying hello,' said Granny.

'I wish they'd say bye-bye,' said Connie.

'Ooh dear,' said Granny, pulling a silly face. 'Someone's nose has been put out of joint by the twins. I think our Connie's gone a bit green-eyed.'

Granny often used odd expressions that Connie didn't understand. Connie went upstairs to the bathroom to give her face a quick check. When she came downstairs again Granny was still talking about her.

'It's just as well the twins have come along. Connie's a dear little girl but she can be a bit of a madam at times.'

'I suppose we have spoilt her rather,' said Dad. 'I've noticed just recently she's becoming very demanding. Always wanting this, wanting that. Trips to Disneyland. House extensions. We're not made of money. Especially now.'

'I hoped Connie would love the twins once they were born,' said Mum. 'I'm going to have to get her to help me more with feeding them and changing and bathing them, that way she'll feel more involved.'

'No, I won't,' Connie muttered.

She sat down on the stairs and hunched up small, her head on her knees. It wasn't fair. They'd all turned on her. They didn't like her any more,

now they'd got the twins.

'Connie?' Mum called. 'Where are you, dear? Connie, could you go and fetch me a clean bib from the airing cupboard, little Claire's dribbled all down hers.'

'Fetch it yourself,' Connie called, crossly.

She knew that would cause trouble. She decided she didn't care. Dad came out into the hall and hissed at her that she was showing them up in front of Granny (and Grandpa and the aunties and assorted friends and neighbours).

'I don't care,' Connie shouted.

Granny came out into the hall then.

'There! Didn't I say she could be a right little madam at times,' said Granny, shaking her head.

'I DON'T CARE!' Connie bawled, louder than both babies together.

It wasn't fair at all. When the babies got cross and cried they got cuddled and fed. When Connie got cross and cried she was given a good talking to and sent up to her bedroom.

Connie lay on her new pink and blue patchwork quilt and wept.

'Connie? Don't cry, pet.'

Mum came into the new bedroom. She'd given one twin to Dad to hold and the other twin to Granny. Her arms were empty at last. She could sit down beside Connie and give her a cuddle after all.

Connie lay snuffling in Mum's arms, feeling very much like a baby herself.

'Want my bockle,' she said, pretending to be a baby.

Mum laughed and pretended to feed her. 'There you are, my little baby,' she said. Then she sat Connie up straight. 'But you're not really a baby, are you, Connie? You're my big girl and you're going to be a good girl, aren't you? You're going to help me look after the twins? They need you to be their lovely big kind sister.'

Connie didn't feel one bit like a lovely big kind sister. Little Charles and Claire might very well need her. But Connie certainly didn't feel she needed *them*.

4 Blue Beads

Connie wasn't sure she wanted to be good. The twins were absolutely sure *they* didn't want to be good. They cried and cried and cried all that night. Mum and Dad were in and out of bed, feeding them and rocking them and changing them. The moment Mum and Dad stopped, the twins started. Most of the time they cried together. Every now and then Charles nodded off but Claire cried louder to make up for it. Then she screamed herself into submission and slept and Charles was startled awake by the silence. He cried. And then Claire woke up all over again and cried too.

Mum was nearly crying by the morning. And Dad. And Connie.

She couldn't find a clean blouse for school because the airing cupboard was chock-full of baby clothes. She couldn't get her hair to go right and Mum was too busy to fix it for her. Connie sighed heavily.

'Those babies kept me awake *all* night,' she complained. 'They kept crying.'

'Goodness. Did they?' said Dad, heavily sarcastic. 'Well, I *am* surprised.'

'Couldn't you feed them or something to keep them quiet?' said Connie.

'I feel as if I've fed five hundred babies,' said Mum.

She put her head down on the breakfast table and her eyelids drooped.

'You need some rest,' said Dad. 'Go back to bed, love. Connie and I will hold the fort until Granny comes.'

'But I'll be late for school,' said Connie.

She didn't really mind being late for school. It was arithmetic first lesson and Miss Peters sometimes got cross if you didn't catch on to things straight away. But Connie felt like being awkward. She really hadn't slept very much last night and so she felt very cross and cranky. Dad was feeling cross and cranky too.

'Do you have to be so difficult, Connie?' he

said, glaring at her.

'Yes,' said Connie, glaring back.

'Now Connie,' said Mum wearily. 'I thought you were going to be a good girl and help us look after the twins?'

'*I* didn't want the twins to come barging into this family and spoiling everything,' said Connie. 'It's not fair. Why should I have to be good all the time? Why do I have to want the twins to be here?'

Charles and Claire started whimpering dismally in their carry-cots, as if they could understand what she was saying.

'Oh dear, they've started again,' said Mum, getting to her feet.

'I'll see to them. You go to bed,' said Dad.

'You're not even listening to me,' said Connie.

'They probably just need changing. They can't need *another* feed,' said Mum.

'I'll take a look,' said Dad, unbuttoning both babies.

'Dad, you're not going to change them in the kitchen?' said Connie, pulling a face. 'Pooh! I'm trying to eat my breakfast.'

'And I'm trying to keep my patience!' said Dad. 'What's *up* with you, Connie? How can you be so rude and selfish? Why can't you help?'

Part of Connie badly wanted to help. She hated Mum and Dad being cross with her. But she was cross, too.

'Nobody asked me whether I wanted the twins. I'm part of this family, aren't I? And now it's all horrid and everyone's cross and you all keep getting on to me. You don't know what it's like for me. I wish there was some way I could make you understand,' Connie wailed.

Just then the doorbell went.

'It'll be Granny,' said Mum thankfully.

But it wasn't Granny. It was the District Nurse, come to check up on Mum and the babies.

'Hello there. I'm Nurse Meade,' she said, smiling.

Connie smiled back, suddenly not feeling so cross. Nurse Meade had a friendly face and a bright blue frock and her long black hair was twisted into dozens of little plaits fastened with tiny blue glass beads.

'Oh, I do like your hair!' said Connie.

'Do you, sweetheart?' said Nurse Meade, bustling into the kitchen and nodding and smiling at Mum and Dad and the two bawling babies. 'Well, tell you what. While Dad carries on changing your new baby brother and sister and Mum pops back to bed I'll give you one little plait of your own, eh?'

She lifted Connie up on to the draining board and twiddled with her hair. It seemed to be only a few seconds before Connie had her own tiny twisted plait bobbing about her ear. Nurse Meade

even fastened it with two of her own blue glass beads.

'There. Don't you look pretty now,' said Nurse Meade, showing Connie her reflection in the kettle. 'You watch out for those blue beads now. They're magic.'

'Magic?' said Connie, laughing. Who was Nurse Meade kidding?

'Magic,' said Nurse Meade, nodding her head vigorously, so that all the blue glass beads on the ends of her own plaits swung and sparkled in the sunlight.

5 New Grannies

Connie didn't think much of Nurse Meade's magic beads. She glanced over at the babies and twiddled one bead wistfully . . . but little Claire and little Charles carried right on crying in their cots.

Connie went off to school with Dad. She was very late and Miss Peters was cross which wasn't at all fair, because it really wasn't Connie's fault. At least Connie had managed to miss half the dreaded arithmetic lesson, but all the children had been told to get into pairs for a measuring and weighing project. Karen was always Connie's partner, but Connie hadn't been there and Karen had paired up with Angela Robinson. Connie couldn't stick Angela Robinson. She went to

ballet and was always showing off all the different dances she could do.

When it was playtime Connie wanted to have a good long moan to Karen about the twins. Karen didn't seem too keen. She wanted to prance about in the playground with Angela.

'That's not fair,' said Connie. 'You're my friend, not Angela's.'

'Yes, well, I want to be Angela's friend too,' said Karen, and she pointed her toes and did a sort of twiddly skip towards Angela.

Connie didn't point her toes and do the twiddly skip. She hunched up in a corner of the playground by herself. She twiddled the blue beads instead of her legs, but wish as she might, Karen and Angela didn't trip mid-twiddle and fall down on their bottoms.

'Magic!' Connie sighed. 'There's no such thing. I didn't *really* believe that Nurse Meade.'

When they went back into the classroom, Angela said in a very loud voice that she thought Connie's hair looked stupid with one silly plait sticking out like that. Karen said she agreed. Connie said nothing at all. She decided she wasn't Karen's friend any more. She didn't seem to be anyone's friend at the moment. Not even Mum and Dad and Granny.

'It's all because of those twins,' Connie brooded. 'They've made everything horrid. And they've made me horrid too, so that no one likes me any more.'

She felt very miserable indeed as she trailed across the playground at going home time. Karen usually came out with her, arm in arm, but Karen was busy arabesquing with Angela. Connie peered round for Granny. She hoped she wouldn't give her a little lecture about being naughty. She didn't *want* to be naughty. Granny didn't understand what it was like.

Connie pulled on her plait, twiddling the blue beads so agitatedly that they clinked together.

33

There was a weird little blue spark at the corner of her eye. Connie blinked. Ah, there was Granny. No, wait a minute. There were two other women pushing in front of her. They were waving and smiling and calling.

'Hello, Connie, sweetheart!'

'Ah, don't you look pretty, pet! Here, would you like some chocolate, darling, I'm sure you're a bit peckish.'

'And we'll buy you an ice cream from the van. A giant 99 with strawberry sauce.'

'We've got a surprise for you too, Connie! We've been busy knitting for our favourite little granddaughter.'

Connie's mouth was wide open in wonder. So was Granny's.

'What . . .? Who . . .?' Granny stammered. Then she recovered a little, and barged between them. 'Now get this straight! Connie is *my* granddaughter.'

'She's our granddaughter too, now.'

'That's right. We're her new twin grannies.'

They smiled twin grins and each took one of Connie's hands.

'But this is ridiculous! You can't possibly be Connie's grannies. She's only got one granny – and that's me!' Granny protested.

'You're her *old* granny.'

'We're her new twin grannies and we're *much* nicer, aren't we, Connie?'

The new twin grannies were remarkably like Connie's real granny. They were the same height as Granny – but they were several stone lighter. They were wearing the same suit as Granny – but theirs looked much smarter. They had the same grey hair as Granny – but they had obviously just been to the hairdresser. They looked quite a lot younger than Granny, too.

Connie didn't know what to say. The twin grannies squeezed her hands, pulling her out of the playground and along the road. Connie's real granny had to trot along behind.

'You like us best, don't you, Connie? Would you like a Mars Bar or a KitKat? No, *I* know, a Mars Bar *and* a KitKat.'

'Of course you like us best. How about a jumbo ice lolly after your ice cream?'

'Yes, please!' said Connie. 'I do like you both. Very much.'

There was a little wail from Connie's real granny as she puffed along the pavement, desperate to keep up.

'Can we slow down a bit?' said Connie. 'My other granny's getting left behind.'

'Good job, too. She's so bossy and bad-tempered.'

'Can't be bothered with you half the time. You don't want her.'

Connie's real granny gave a moan and stumbled, nearly falling.

'Granny!' said Connie. She stopped. She swung her arms and snatched her hands away from the new twin grannies. 'I like you. Well, I think I do. But I like my other granny, too. I like her just as much as you.'

'Oh, Connie!' said Granny and she straightened herself up and hugged Connie tight. They had a very long and loving hug. And when they looked up at last the new twin grannies had gone.

6 Purple Puddles

Granny bought Connie an ice cream from the van on the way home from school. A giant 99 with strawberry sauce. She didn't mention a jumbo lolly or a Mars Bar or a KitKat but Connie knew she'd better not push her luck.

'Thanks ever so, Granny,' she said, licking happily.

'You'd better not tell your mum,' said Granny.

Connie and Granny looked at each other. Connie decided Granny didn't mean the ice cream. Granny glanced over her shoulder, checking that there was no one else around. Especially not another granny or two.

'Course I won't tell,' said Connie, slurping up strawberry sauce.

She felt quite a lot better. When they got home Connie called out a chirpy, 'Hi there, Mum,' the moment she got in the front door.

'Sh!' Mum hissed.

'Waaaaa!' wailed Charles.

'Waaaaa!' wailed Claire.

'Oh no,' said Mum. 'For goodness sake, Connie! I'd just spent the last twenty minutes rocking them, trying to get them to nod off. And now you've got them started all over again.'

'I only said hello,' said Connie, wounded. 'I didn't know the babies were asleep.'

'Well, they're certainly not asleep now,' Mum said grimly.

'I'll see to them, dear,' said Granny. 'Then I'd better get home to Grandpa. Connie, you go and put the kettle on, there's a darling. I'm sure Mum could do with a cup of tea.'

Connie went into the kitchen and plugged in the kettle. She decided to be really helpful even though Mum hadn't been very welcoming. She laid the tray with cups and saucers and set out some biscuits from the tin. She nibbled a biscuit or two herself as she was feeling peckish, in spite of the giant 99 ice cream.

The twins were still yelling furiously in the other room. They sounded more than a bit peckish themselves.

Connie fixed herself a drink of blackcurrant juice. Karen's baby sister Susie loved blackcurrant juice. She'd glug so much she generally looked as if she was wearing purple lipstick. Maybe baby Charles and baby Claire might fancy a drink of juice?

Connie fished out two baby bottles from the sterilizing unit and filled them up with diluted blackcurrant juice. The bottles were a bit fiddly, and she had a job fixing on the rubber teats. Her fingers slipped, her hand shook . . . and suddenly there was a crash. The bottle didn't break but as it skidded across the kitchen floor it sprayed purple juice all over everything.

'What was that?' Mum called, and she came hurrying into the kitchen. She didn't look where she was going and stepped right into a purple puddle.

'What on earth . . . ? Oh Connie!'

'I was just trying to help, Mum,' said Connie.

'Oh yes, this is a big help,' said Mum, crossly, getting the floor mop. 'Why were you playing around with the babies' bottles? I shall have to scrub them out and sterilize them all over again.'

'I thought they'd like a drink of blackcurrant juice, that's all,' said Connie.

'Oh, don't be so silly, Connie, they're far too little for that sort of drink. Why couldn't you just do as you were told?'

'You told me you wanted me to help you,' said Connie.

'Well, now I'm telling you to leave well alone,' said Mum, wringing out the sticky purple cloth and dabbing at the stains on her slippers.

'All right,' said Connie, and she flounced off upstairs.

It wasn't fair. She hadn't dropped the wretched bottle on purpose. She couldn't seem to do anything right. Mum didn't even seem to want to talk to her any more.

Connie flopped onto her bed, moodily picking at the patches on her quilt. She remembered she wasn't talking to Karen either. Karen and Angela had gone off together after school. She couldn't understand what Karen saw in that awful Angela.

'She looks really daft when she dances,' Connie mumbled to herself.

She got up off the bed to do an imitation of Angela dancing, sticking out her feet and waggling her bottom rather a lot. She caught sight of herself in her mirror and giggled. She attempted several Angela-style leaps in the air, and landed with a thump.

There was a distant wail. And another.

'*Connie!*' Mum sounded very cross indeed. 'Whatever are you doing now? How dare you jump about like that! You've woken the twins *again*. Are you being deliberately naughty?'

'No!' said Connie, flinging herself back on her bed.

She was in trouble again and it really wasn't fair. She wasn't being naughty. Mum didn't understand.

Connie buried her head in her pillow. She fiddled with her hair for comfort. Her fingers found her new little plait. She twiddled the two blue beads and they clinked together and even in the dark depths of her pillow Connie saw a strange blue spark . . .

7 Fun Mums

There was a knock on Connie's bedroom door.
Two knocks. 'Are you in there, Connie dear?'

'May we come in, poppet?'

Connie sat up straight. She swallowed.

'Who is it?' she called, tentatively.

'It's Mum, darling.'

'Surely you know your own mum?'

Two twin mums stepped into Connie's bedroom
and smiled at her. They looked a lot like her own
old mum, but these twins were much more glittery
and glossy. They were both wearing Mum's sparkly
sequined evening dress and they were wearing
Mum's rings and bracelets and necklaces all at
once, so that they jingled as they walked. They'd
sprayed on so much flowery scent that Connie
sneezed.

'Do you like our perfume, darling?'

'Would you like a little squirt, mmm?'

They produced twin bottles and sprayed Connie's neck and wrists, while she wriggled and giggled.

'Connie?' It was Connie's own ordinary Mum calling up the stairs. 'Connie, what are you up to now? What's that smell? You're not playing around with my birthday present perfume, are you?'

'No, Mum,' Connie called truthfully.

Mum wasn't convinced. She came plodding purposefully up the stairs.

'Connie, I'm getting very cross with you. You're telling me fibs, aren't you? The whole house *reeks* of perfume.'

She barged into Connie's bedroom and then stood stock-still in her stained slippers, staring at the new twin mothers.

'Who are you?' she gasped.

'We're Connie's new twin mums, of course.'

'Don't you ever knock when you come into our Connie's bedroom?'

'She's not your Connie. She's mine!'

'Oh, you're only her old mum. She's got us now.'

'We're much much nicer, aren't we, Connie? Here, would you like to play Grown-up Ladies,

sweetie? Try stepping out in my high heels.'

She kicked off her glittery dance shoes and Connie tried them on, staggering a few steps across her carpet.

'Those are my shoes!' said Mum. 'Take them off at once, Connie. I told you, you'll twist your ankle.'

'She's all gloom and doom, that old mum of yours, isn't she, Connie? We're much more fun.'

'Would you like to mess about with our make-up, darling? You'd look so cute with a little lipstick and eyeshadow.'

'Look, will you stop this nonsense!' Mum shouted. 'You can't come bursting into my house and taking over my daughter like this. I'm Connie's mum and that's my make-up and that's my best evening dress you're wearing. And I don't know how, but *you're* wearing it, too. So both of you, take it off!'

'But it doesn't fit *you* any more, does it?'

'You've got *much* too fat.'

'*We* stick to our diet and fitness programme.'

'Cottage cheese and celery sticks and aerobics every day!'

'Am I going to have to eat cottage cheese and celery too?' said Connie, smearing blue eyeshadow on her lids and then blinking up at her new twin mums.

'Of course not, sweetheart. You're a growing girl. We'll cook you your favourite spaghetti bolognese every day, and you can have strawberry pavlova for pudding. Your old mum only gives you that on your birthday, doesn't she?'

'Look, I'm worn out and rushed off my feet at the moment, I haven't got time to cook,' said Mum, miserably.

'We *make* time. And we're much much much busier than you.'

'That's right. We go out to work. We have our own office and we earn lots of money.'

'So did I, once. But the twins are so little, they

47

need me at home,' said Mum. 'And Connie needs me too, don't you, Connie?' She looked at Connie rather desperately.

'Of course I need you, Mum,' said Connie, putting a lipstick smile on her face.

'But she needs us more. You can't be in two places at once. *We* can. One of us can go out to work and one of us can stay home and chat to Connie, easy peasy.'

'Those babies are bawling downstairs. You'd better go and see what they want now.'

The twin mums took hold of her and turned her towards the door.

'But what does Connie want?' said Mum, struggling.

'I want you, Mum,' said Connie, and she pushed past the two twin mums and pulled her own mum free of them.

They cuddled up close on Connie's bed and they didn't even notice the twin mothers sliding out of the door.

8 Best Friends

'I don't think I'm ever going to squeeze into this again,' said Mum, sighing. She'd found her own sparkly evening dress at the back of her wardrobe and was holding it up against herself. 'You might as well have it for dressing up, Connie,' said Mum, handing it to her.

'Oh, Mum! Really? Wow!' said Connie, jumping up and down.

'And I'll find you some of my make-up – just the old bits and pieces, mind, not any of my good stuff – and we can make you up properly if you want. You look like a clown at the moment,' said Mum, rubbing at Connie's face with a tissue.

Connie pulled on Mum's frock over her T-shirt and perched on a chair while Mum started fussing

around her, pretending to be a lady in a beauty salon.

'What colour eyeshadow would Madam like?' Mum asked, but as Connie was choosing there was a cry from downstairs. Then another.

Mum looked at Connie. Connie looked at Mum.

'Well, they'll just have to cry for five minutes. We're busy,' said Mum.

She made up one of Connie's eyes very carefully, while the crying continued downstairs.

'It's okay, Mum. I'll do the other one,' said Connie. 'You'd better go and feed the twins again.'

'They're going to get as fat as elephants at this rate,' said Mum. 'They'll be growing trunks and trumpeting next. Sorry to interrupt the game, Connie. Here, tell you what – why don't you phone Karen and ask her to come round and play dressing up with you?'

'Oh yes,' said Connie. And then she remembered. 'Oh no,' she said instead.

'What's up?' said Mum.

'Karen and I aren't friends any more,' said Connie.

'Well, why don't you phone her up and make friends?' said Mum.

'I'm not sure she likes me any more. And anyway, she's probably playing round at that awful Angela's,' said Connie. 'She wants to be her friend now.'

'Why can't you all be friends?' said Mum.

Connie raised her newly painted eyebrow expressively.

But she rang Karen all the same. She felt shy and squirmy inside at first, as if Karen was a stranger.

'Do you want to come round to my house to play?' she blurted out. She was worried Karen might say no or make some excuse. But Karen seemed quite happy about the idea, thank goodness.

'Bring some dressing-up clothes and some of your mum's old make-up,' said Connie. She was about to hang up the phone. She hesitated. 'And you can bring Angela, too, if you really want.'

'She's gone off to her ballet class. She's a bit miffed with me, actually. I accidentally kicked her when I was copying one of those twiddly things she does with her leg stuck out, and she didn't half carry on about it. I think she takes all that dancing stuff far too seriously.'

Karen only lived ten minutes' walk away so she and Connie were soon playing dressing-up. They didn't take it seriously at all. They strutted around in long frocks and smiled silly smiles and shrieked with laughter at each other's antics. It didn't matter about making a noise because the twins were awake anyway, being fed and changed.

'Can I have a quick look at them?' asked Karen, when it was time for her to go home.

She'd already seen the twins when they came straight from the hospital and had privately agreed with Connie that they didn't look a patch on her baby sister Susie.

But now when Karen saw Claire and Charles, temporarily pink and peaceful in Mum's arms, she seemed impressed.

'Oh, don't they look sweet like that!' Karen whispered.

'Sweet?' Connie whispered back, staring at her baby brother and sister.

'You are lucky, Connie. I wish Susie had been twins,' said Karen. 'Look at them, they're as good as gold. I thought you said they cried all the time.'

'They do, don't they, Mum?' said Connie.

'It certainly seems like it,' said Mum. 'You're not good at all, are you, twins? You're big bad babies who bully us something rotten.'

Baby Claire and baby Charles blinked blue eyes, all innocence.

Karen laughed and said goodbye.

'If you're late to school again tomorrow I'll wait for you,' said Karen. 'I won't be Angela's partner again. I've gone off her.'

'I was scared you might have gone off me,' said Connie. 'We are still best friends, aren't we, Karen?'

'You bet, bestest friends ever,' said Karen.

They linked little fingers and vowed that they would never break friends again.

9 Growly Bears

Dad was very late home. The car had broken down and he was in a bad mood because it was going to cost a lot of money to get it mended.

'Karen's dad's got a new car,' said Connie.

'Well, *your* dad's got to make do with a very very old car,' said Dad, bitterly.

'It would be nice to have a new car,' said Connie. She was simply making conversation but it seemed to irritate Dad.

'Well, we can't have a new car so there's no point asking,' said Dad, though Connie had done no such thing. Then he took a close look at her. 'What's all that muck on your face, Connie?'

'Make-up, Dad.'

'*Make-up*? Whatever's going on? You're much

much too young to wear make-up!'

'It's just for dressing up, Dad. I wouldn't wear it out.'

'You go and give your face a wash this minute.'

'Oh, Dad. It looks lovely. I want to leave it on. And Karen's mum lets her wear pink lip gloss even when she goes out.'

'Connie.' Dad was starting to look very cross. 'I don't want to hear another word about Karen. Or Karen's mum. Or Karen's dad. Or any other member of Karen's family.'

'Karen's baby sister, Susie,' said Connie helpfully, because she was the only one Dad hadn't mentioned.

Dad didn't find this helpful. He seemed to think she was being deliberately cheeky.

'That's enough,' he said, firmly. 'Go and wash your face at once. And then get ready for bed.'

'But it's not my bedtime yet!' said Connie, indignantly. 'Mum, it's not fair, Dad says I've got to go to bed and yet it's not my bedtime for another twenty minutes.'

'If you're not upstairs in *twenty seconds* then you will seriously regret it, young lady,' Dad bellowed.

His shouts seriously upset the twins, who both started bawling. Connie practically burst into tears herself. Her face was all screwed up as she ran up the stairs, and when she was in the bathroom a few tears spurted down her cheeks. Blue tears, because of the blue eyeshadow still on her eyelids. The shiny blue tears made her remember her two shiny blue beads.

'It's not fair,' Connie said, sniffling. 'Dad can shout all he wants and wake up the babies and *he* doesn't get told off. And I've got into trouble over nothing! I was being good, for goodness sake. It wouldn't be so bad if I was being bad, but I wasn't!'

She twiddled the beads in her little plait and they clinked together. There was a blue flash in the bathroom. Then a knock at the door. Two knocks.

'Who's that?' said Connie – although she knew perfectly well who it was going to be.

But there was no answer. The knocking got louder. There was a sort of scratching at the door. And then a growl.

'What's that?' Connie called, shivering.

'A great big ferocious growly bear coming to hug you to death!'

'Two big ferocious growly bears coming to gobble up their little girl!'

The bathroom door burst open and Connie squealed as twin dads rushed into the room, growling and grunting.

'Grrrr!'

'Grrrr!'

'Help! Don't! Oooh! Tee-heeeee!' Connie screamed, as they picked her up in their pretend paws and tickled her with their pretend claws.

'Connie? What's the matter? Why are you screaming? Hang on, Dad's coming!' Dad shouted from downstairs.

He came running into the bathroom and bumped right into the twin dads and Connie.

'Get off my daughter!' Dad yelled, and he tried to drag Connie free.

'She's our daughter, too!'

'We're having a game. Connie loves a romp, don't you, darling?'

'You haven't played with Connie for ages.'

'You just get cross with her when the poor kid hasn't even done anything.'

'I don't know what you two creeps are playing at, but *I'm* Connie's father!' Dad shouted.

'We're playing growly bears, eh, Connie? Grrrr!'

'And you call yourself a father, when you're no fun at all. Grrrr!'

'Will you stop this! Get away from my Connie. Get out of this bathroom, do you hear?' Dad bellowed, and he tried to push them out.

It was a mistake. The twin dads were quite a bit bigger and they had much broader shoulders.

'Who are you shoving, eh?'

'Getting all hot and bothered! You need to cool down a bit.'

They picked Dad up and tipped him in the bath.

'I'll hold him down while you turn on the tap!'

'He could do with a swim!'

'Don't really,' said Connie.

'I don't know why you're sticking up for him. He never sticks up for you.'

'And he hasn't taken you for a proper swim for ages, has he?'

'It's not Dad's fault,' said Connie. She couldn't bear to see Dad stuck in the bath like that. 'Here, Dad. I'll help you out,' she said, and she took hold of his hands and pulled with all her might.

Dad shot upwards so rapidly that Connie fell backwards, bowling the twin dads over.

'Connie? Are you all right?' Dad asked, picking her up and hugging her even harder than a big ferocious growly bear.

The twin dads went on bowling right out of the bathroom, down the stairs, out of the door, out of sight.

10 Baby Blue-Eyes

Dad tucked Connie up in bed that night. He pretended she was still little and tucked all her old dolls and her big battered teddy in with her. He made the dolls talk in silly little twittery voices and he made the teddy growl. The growling made both of them look up and check the door, just to make sure no one else was coming to join in the game.

'It's just us, Dad,' said Connie. 'And Mum downstairs.'

'And the babies,' said Dad.

'Yep. The twins,' said Connie.

'I suppose it's been very weird for you, Connie. I bet it must have seemed like the twins were taking over at times,' said Dad.

'Mmm,' said Connie.

'I think it'll take a while before we all get used to being a family of five. We're all tired out at the moment because the little blighters keep us awake half the night, but once they get a bit older it should get easier. If more expensive,' said Dad, sighing a little.

'Poor Dad. It's not fair you've got to work more.'

'Oh, I'll manage. Though I do miss our Saturday morning swim. Tell you what, Connie. How about if we go swimming on Sunday mornings instead? Just you and me. Would you like that?'

'You bet,' said Connie.

'Night night then, poppet,' said Dad.

Mum tiptoed in from the twins' room to say

goodnight, too. She sat on one side of Connie's bed, and Dad sat on the other. They had a grand family cuddle, just like they had in the old days. Before the twins.

Perhaps Charles and Claire felt left out. There was a little snorty sound. A snuffle. And then two plaintive cries.

'Oh-oh,' said Mum.

'Oh-oh,' said Dad.

'Oh-oh,' said Connie.

They all laughed, and then Mum and Dad went off to deal with a twin each and Connie curled up and went to sleep. She'd forgotten to undo the little plait. As she turned this way and that the beads bumped her head and stuck in uncomfortably. Connie mumbled in her sleep and fiddled with her plait. One blue bead slid off. Then the other. The plait unravelled and the two beads rolled across the pillow, off the bed, over the rug and disappeared down a crack in the floorboards.

Connie woke up early the next morning. She could hear an occasional car going by in the road outside. She could hear a few sparrows singing in the garden. She could hear the hum of a milk float. She could hear Dad snoring in the room further down the landing. She could hear Mum sigh sleepily as she turned over in bed. But she couldn't hear anything else.

She couldn't hear the twins. They'd both been roaring their heads off long before this, yesterday. Connie waited. Still no sound. Not a wail, not a whimper. She sat up in bed and scratched her head. Her fingers slipped through her hair. She realised the plait had gone, and the two blue beads. The beads had proved very magical indeed, after all.

Connie remembered what she had half wished when Nurse Meade first gave her the beads . . . She wondered if she might accidentally have clinked them together in the night. Maybe the beads could really take away twins as well as adding them?

Connie shot out of bed and ran into the twins' room. She charged to their cots, feeling sick with terror. Just for a moment she couldn't spot the two small heads on their pillows. But then she blinked and the teary blur went and she saw Claire in one cot, Charles in the other.

Connie skidded to a halt, breathing a huge sigh of relief. It only made a little whistling sound in the room but it was enough to waken one of the babies. Claire. She made a tiny yowling sound like a kitten and opened her eyes. They were big and

63

blue, almost as blue as the beads. They seemed to be looking right up at Connie.

'Hello, little sister,' Connie whispered.

Charles woke up, too. He did it differently, screwing up his face and smacking his small lips together before opening his eyes. They were big and bead-blue, too and they blinked when Connie bent over him.

'Hello, little brother,' Connie whispered.

She waited for them to start crying. But they seemed surprisingly content to lie on their backs and look at her. Connie looked back at them.

'Maybe you're not so bad after all, little babies,' said Connie.

She stood between the cots, letting her hands dangle. She gently stroked their poor little bald heads. She felt very soft down. Maybe they'd soon get to be curly after all. She touched their tiny button noses and tickled them under their chins. They didn't laugh but they looked as if they wanted to, if they only knew how. Then she played with their small starfish hands. Claire gripped her tightly round the left little finger. Charles clung to her right little finger, his fist clenched.

'Make friends?' said Connie.